The dolls' house stands in the nursery,
its front door always waiting to be
opened. Elizabeth Small, who knows
how to magically make herself
doll-size, knocks on the door and
joins the fun inside.

As usual, Elizabeth finds the
household humming with excitement.
Vanessa, the bossy doll, is playing
hairdresser and manages to wash the
hair right off the head of Jacqueline,
the saucy French doll! Then there is
little Lupin who has trouble with
words, silly Amanda who clashes the
saucepans out of time when the girls
form a band, and Jane who becomes
a poetess.

The unpredictable escapades of these
fun-loving dolls and their friends—
the mischievous monkey, the black
kitten, the copycat parrot, and baby
Robin—provide many hilarious
moments.

Is A Flower: *The Life of George
Washington Carver,* and Hush
Little Baby: *A Folk Lullaby.* She
is a graduate of the Museum College
of Art in Philadelphia and now lives
in New York City. She and her
husband Franz have a young son,
Jason, and a baby daughter, Alexa.

HELEN CLARE

FIVE DOLLS AND THEIR FRIENDS

ILLUSTRATED BY ALIKI

PRENTICE-HALL, Inc., Englewood Cliffs, New Jersey

For Jill

Five Dolls and Their Friends, by Helen Clare

First published in the U.S.A. by Prentice-Hall, Inc., Englewood Cliffs, N.J., 1968

First published in Great Britain by The Bodley Head, 1959

© by Helen Clare, 1959

© by Aliki Brandenberg, 1968, for illustrations in this edition

Printed in the United States of America

Library of Congress Catalog Card Number: 68-10650
J32102

CONTENTS

I

HUNDREDS
AND THOUSANDS

ELIZABETH had not visited her dolls for so long that she was afraid they might be offended. First she had been ill with a sore throat, then she had had her tonsils out, and then she had been sent away to her aunt in the country to get better. She decided that she must take the inhabitants of the dolls' house a treat to make up.

She wondered what it should be. Perhaps they would like something to eat best of all, as she often did herself. In the kitchen, her mother had been decorating cakes with those tiny, tiny round balls called hundreds and thousands, all colours. These, thought Elizabeth, were just right for the dolls! Why hadn't she thought of them before? Once she had taken silver pills, but the dolls thought they were marbles or beads, and anyway when they ate them they almost choked. She tipped the rest of the hundreds and thousands into a paper bag, and screwed it up tightly.

In the nursery stood the dolls' house, its windows winking at her and its front door closed, but waiting to be opened. The dolls' house always looked inviting.

She turned herself small in the way which only she knew, and which had been told her once by the monkey who lived on the roof. Then she ran up the path and knocked at the door.

At first there was no answer.

Elizabeth opened the letter-box and peered through. From the dining-room she could hear Vanessa's voice. It was the voice she put on when people called or when she spoke on the telephone. Vanessa was the eldest doll.

She knocked again.

There was a patter, and the dining-room door opened a bit further. Then there were a great many whispers and shushes.

"Dear, oh dear," Elizabeth heard Vanessa say. "What a moment to call, whoever it is, just when I am on the telephone——"

"You're not *on* it, Vanessa," whispered Lupin's voice. Lupin was the youngest doll.

"Don't argue! Hold the line, hold the line, please!" Elizabeth heard Vanessa say. "Now, quickly, someone go and answer the door!"

"It hasn't said anything yet," remarked Lupin.

"You ridiculous doll, let Jane go."

Elizabeth saw Jane coming, and stood up quickly.

"Mrs. Small!" said Jane, throwing the door wide open.

Jane was a sweet and gentle doll, always pleased to see everyone, and always polite. She wore a long green night-dress. Although she had once made herself a new dress, she seemed to like the old one best.

"Mrs. Small! Mrs. Small!" whispered all the other dolls. Little Lupin, wearing only her knitted vest which seemed to have more stitches dropped than ever, ran and took Elizabeth's hand. Amanda, the fair-haired, cheeky doll, rushed to the other side, giggling.

"Come on, we're telephoning, it's such fun," she whispered. "Hurry, or silly old Vanessa will be cross."

"Hullo, Jacqueline," said Elizabeth to her French doll, who stood near the dining-room door. (Vanessa always called her the paying-guest.)

"'Allo!" she said, winking.

"You have to whisper, or Vanessa can't hear," explained Jane, doing so.

The dolls led Elizabeth into the dining-room. There sat Vanessa, the red-cheeked, bossy doll, holding on to the telephone and trying hard to smile. But it was plain that she was cross and did not like being disturbed.

"Come in, come in, dear landlady," she hissed, "we are very glad to see you, but I can't say you have come at the right moment this time, for I am on the telephone——"

"Vanessa keeps saying she's *on* it. She isn't *on* it, is she?" said Lupin again.

"I am on the telephone," said Vanessa, looking sternly at Lupin, "to the grocer. The fact is, Mrs. Small, there is a cupboard under the dresser in the kitchen——"

"Why is it called the dresser if it doesn't dress?" Lupin asked. "I've never seen it wear a dress at all."

"I've never seen you wear a dress either," Vanessa snapped, "so perhaps you'll be quiet and not interrupt. As I was saying, Mrs. Small, the cupboard is quite bare like Mother Hubbard's, which can't be right, so genteel as we all are, such ladies as we were brought up. So I am ordering some groceries for it, to come by telephone, so simple. The shop had just answered when you unfortunately came to the door——"

"I'm *so* sorry, Vanessa," Elizabeth said.

"Anyway a shop can't answer," said Amanda naughtily. "Shops don't speak, and neither do doors, so there."

"I asked the grocer to hold on," said Vanessa, blushing, "so I hope he has done so. Hullo, hullo!" she said loudly.

"Hold on to what?" Lupin asked Elizabeth.

"Shush!" she said anxiously.

"Hullo! Ah! Good. Forgive me keeping you waiting . . . you keeping me waiting. . . ." Vanessa said getting muddled, "but shops are there to oblige . . . here is the list, I will read it out. . . ." Vanessa beckoned to Jane and Jane brought a piece of paper.

Elizabeth looked over Jane's shoulder and saw that it said SHOPPING LIST. On it Jane had written down a great many things.

"Ready? Now, Jane," Vanessa whispered, "you read it, as you know what you have written, and I haven't my spectacles."

"She can't read," jeered the monkey's voice down the chimney.

"Hold the line! Hold the line!" said the parrot in the gilt cage, suddenly.

Jane coughed.

"Just make it up, Vanessa," she said.

"Very well, since we can't keep them waiting any longer. A pat of butter," she began loudly, "a packet of tea, a tin of cough drops, half a pound of twopenny rice, half a pound of treacle."

"That's the way the money goes, pop goes the weasel," sang the monkey down the chimney.

Vanessa took no notice.

"A mile of macaroni," she said wildly, "a yard of candles, a lot of sugar, an apple each. . . ."

"He won't know how many there are of you!" whispered Elizabeth.

"Hush, Mrs. Small, he's a very clever grocer

and used to numbers. A hundred eggs——"

"Ooh, Vanessa!" Amanda said, "we can have scrambled eggs."

"That *is* a lot," said Jane doubtfully.

"Nonsense. A million sweets——"

"Goodee, goodee," said Lupin, jumping.

"Yum, yum," said Jacqueline, who certainly knew the word sweets.

"A sack of flour and a stone of potatoes," finished Vanessa in triumph.

It was a very strange order.

"That will be all. . . . Yes, as soon as ever you can. . . . We shall be here to receive them. . . . Good-bye. . . . Thank you. . . ."

She put down the telephone, smiling broadly, and her feather bobbed.

"There!" she said. "Now all we have to do is to sit here and wait till they come through and catch them. Could anything be easier?"

"Come *through,* Vanessa?" said Elizabeth.

"Through the letter-box?" asked Jane, anxiously, thinking of the sack of flour.

"Through the window, I expect," Amanda suggested. "Let's open it."

"Yes, because the stony potatoes will break the glass," added Lupin.

"Why, you ridiculous dolls, they are coming by telephone, aren't they? They will simply come through the telephone receiver and we shall receive them, so all go and get things to catch them in, as otherwise we shall have a mess on the carpet, and as it is I fear the treacle may be a little sticky——"

Elizabeth shrieked with laughter.

"Vanessa" she said, "they'll send them in a van, to the door. They can't send them over the telephone!"

Vanessa looked astonished and then disappointed, and then angry. Her feather bobbed.

"Then people should say what they mean. I once heard you say quite plainly that your mother ordered the things to come over the telephone, so of course I thought——"

Poor Vanessa went very red, and she stalked out of the room, and her shoulders looked spikier than ever, and her wooden feet made a cross noise on the floor.

Suddenly Elizabeth remembered the sweets. She ran after Vanessa, and took her arm, feeling sorry that she had laughed at her.

"Come and see what I brought you," she said, in an inviting voice.

"What, Mrs. Small?" said Amanda, running after them.

"May we to eat it?" said Jacqueline greedily.

"That paying-guest!" Vanessa sniffed. "Her English is *no* better than when she came, and neither are her manners."

"Where is it?" asked Jane.

"Mrs. Small always brings something," said Lupin happily. "Isn't it nice?"

"Not 'alf," said the monkey's voice above them.

"Not 'alf, not 'alf," echoed the parrot from the dining-room.

Outside the door stood the big white bag, screwed at the top.

"Bring it round to the back garden," said Elizabeth. "Mind, don't tip it, or they'll come out."

The dolls seized the paper bag, and hurried round to the lawn at the back.

"Now!" said Elizabeth. Everybody stood round, looking most excited, even Vanessa. The monkey had moved to the edge of the roof, and was watching with interest.

"You'll never guess what it is, so I'll tell you. It's hundreds and thousands!" Elizabeth said.

There was a puzzled silence.

"Hundreds and thousands of *what*?" said Lupin.

"For once," said Vanessa firmly, "I agree with Lupin. Hundreds and thousands of *what*?"

"Well, they're just called hundreds and thousands because there are so many of them you can't count them, and that's what's so nice——" and Elizabeth began to untwist the bag.

Vanessa put her hands on her hips and snorted.

"It would only be nice," she said, "if they were nice things. You wouldn't want hundreds and thousands of beetles, for instance, or smuts——"

"Or germs!" said Jane nervously.

"Or worms!" said Amanda who liked things to rhyme.

"Or burglars," shivered Jacqueline, who had just learnt the word.

"Or monkeys," said Vanessa loudly, tossing her head in the direction of the roof.

"Or Vanessas," retorted the monkey in a croaky voice.

"Or rice puddings," sighed L pin.

"Be quiet all of you, they're SWEETS!"

Elizabeth said. "I heard you order a million sweets, you see, so——"

"Well, why didn't you say so sooner, dear Mrs. Small, we should have been delighted to receive sweets!" Vanessa said, clasping her hands.

"I toss them in the air, and you all scramble for them," Elizabeth explained.

"Hooray!" said Amanda.

"Really, Mrs. Small, there's enough scrambling in this house without your arranging any more," Vanessa said, "and anyway we're not eggs." But all the same she ran back and stood ready.

The monkey swung quickly down from the roof by means of the fire-escape. It was what the dolls used also as a washing-line, and sometimes as a trapeze to swing on. Really, it was Elizabeth's red dressing-gown cord, which stretched from a chimney pot to the bottom of the garden, where the stable was.

"I'm going to scramble too," he said.

"You were not invited," Vanessa said haughtily.

"I was invited," he said, "by me."

"Isn't he funny," said Amanda. "Come on, Mrs. Small, do begin."

Elizabeth plunged her arm into the bag, which was almost as tall as she was, and seized a handful of the coloured sweets.

"Ready? Go!" she said, and she flung the handful up in the air as high as she could. They came down all over the garden with a pattering noise, on to the green velvet lawn, on to the piece of glass which was called the skating-rink, into the plant pots and the deck chair and the little thatched bird-table, and the stable at the bottom where the mice lived who pulled the mouse-and-trap. The mice peered out and blinked with surprise.

"Oh, how lovely!" said Amanda seizing the sweets and eating them.

"What pretty colours!" said Jane, who was collecting them and putting them in her pockets.

"Can we eat them all now?" said Lupin, sliding across the skating-rink on her hands and knees, as the sweets rolled over it.

"Certainly not," Vanessa said with her mouth full, "it will spoil your dinner." She was lying flat under the deck chair, her shiny feet in the air.

"Strike me pink," yelled the monkey, sweeping up the sweets with his huge hands.

The paying-guest said nothing, for she was much too busy scrambling.

"Here comes another lot!" called Elizabeth, throwing handful after handful, as her father had done for them once with toffees at a party.

"Goodness gracious me, like a hail storm," said Vanessa breathlessly.

The black velvet kitten came out of the back door and darted in a frenzy after the rolling sweets, not knowing which to chase first. They all looked so funny, crawling, running and scrambling over the garden, bumping into each other, and cramming their mouths full, that Elizabeth could hardly throw for laughing. At least they had forgotten the groceries, she thought.

And at last the bag was empty.

"Lupin's got more than me," wailed Amanda.

"I haven't. You've eaten all yours!" said Lupin.

"Hoity-toity," said the monkey, who had caught this saying from the parrot, and liked it.

"You have!"

"Nonsense," Vanessa said, getting up. "You heard Mrs. Small say you can't count them, so how can you possibly tell?" And she bobbed

down again and went on searching. Vanessa was
often very clever at stopping quarrels.

"I've got to go now," Elizabeth called, "but I
shall come again soon, now I'm better."

"Better?" said Vanessa. "Have you been
worse?"

"I've been ill," said Elizabeth, laughing.

"Oh, poor Mrs. Small, we never asked how
you were," said Jane, running up to her.

"You couldn't as you didn't know. I've been
to hospital and had an operation."

At this the dolls all crowded round, staring.

"What's that?" Lupin and Amanda said together.

"They took my tonsils out."

Vanessa looked shocked.

"Where did they take them from?" she said.

"My throat," said Elizabeth.

"Bless my soul, it's a wonder you can speak at
all," Vanessa said.

"I couldn't at first," said Elizabeth, "But I had
lots of ice-cream to make it better. It was
lovely."

"Oh, Mrs. Small, how lucky you are!" said all
the dolls with longing.

"Good-bye," said Elizabeth. "I'm glad you
liked the scramble."

"Oh we did, thank you! Good-bye, dear Mrs. Small!"

"Good-bye, good-bye!"

"Excuse us going on hunting!" sang Vanessa. And she twirled her hand in the air and began to sing in her quavery voice:

"A-hunting we will go
A-hunting we will go,
We'll catch a fox. . . ."

But she stopped here, for this didn't seem suitable.

And as Elizabeth went, they all dropped down again on their hands and knees, looking for more sweets.

The monkey had swung back to the roof. His mouth was so full of sweets that he could only wave, with both arms, as she went.

II

OPERATIONS

Eᴌɪᴢᴀʙᴇᴛʜ thought that the dolls must have some groceries to fill up that kitchen cupboard, so she started to save things to put them in. Whenever her mother threw away a small bottle, she kept its lid and washed it. She cut the corners off paper bags, to make little screw packets. She made two small sacks out of scraps.

17

One of them she filled with flour and tied it up with cotton. She made some knobbly potatoes out of raw pastry her mother gave her, rolled them in cocoa, and put them in the other sack. She put rice and tea and sugar and sweets and macaroni in the packets, some butter and treacle and currants in the lids, and lots of other things that she found in her mother's cupboard. The nicest thing of all was a small bottle of orangeade, a sample from the grocer's. It would be too big of course, but the dolls would love it. She loaded all these goods onto her brother Edward's red lorry, and wheeled it up to the dolls' house gate.

The monkey looked gloomily at her as she walked up the path.

"No visitors today," he said hoarsely.

"Why not?" asked Elizabeth in surprise.

"It ain't visiting day. Visiting days is Wednesdays and Saturdays only, I hears 'em talking about it."

"That sounds like a hospital!"

"It is a 'ospital. Wot's that red thing, the ambulance? They must be very weak, they haven't moved for ages, and they're talking in whispers and croaks."

"Goodness," said Elizabeth, in alarm.

She did not bother to knock at the door, but walked straight in and up the stairs. Vanessa's room was empty and so was the parlour. She went on up to the top landing on tiptoe, and peeped into the paying-guest's room. Jacqueline was not there; what was even stranger, nor was Jacqueline's bed. Across the landing was Jane's room: but that was empty too. Where were all the beds? And what were the dolls doing?

But at this minute a hoarse voice croaked from the room beyond Jane's, where Lupin and Amanda slept.

"Look out, get into bed, here comes the doctor!"

"It isn't, it's me," said Elizabeth loudly, walking in. She couldn't help laughing at them: they had pushed all four beds, and Robin the baby's cradle, into a row in one room, and they were all sitting up in bed with bandages round their throats.

"Mrs. Small, Mrs. Small," squawked Amanda in a hoarse whisper, "we've made a hospital. This is the ward, and we're all waiting to have our tonsils taken out!"

"Our throats are so sore we had to tie them up," whispered Lupin.

"The fact is, Mrs. Small," croaked Vanessa,

"the doctor has been once, and we thought you were he back again. He says we have all caught it and he's bringing the surgeon. To take out the tonsils."

"It's not catching," laughed Elizabeth, watching Vanessa's feather bob angrily. "Vanessa, you can't wear your hat in bed in hospital," she said, to change the subject. "They wouldn't let you."

Vanessa sniffed.

"Where's Jacqueline?" asked Elizabeth.

"She didn't understand," whispered Jane anxiously, "and anyway we had to borrow her bed because we couldn't get Vanessa's four-poster up here, so there wasn't room for her. We don't know where she is."

"And we don't care," said Vanessa firmly.

"Mrs. Small," Amanda said, "could you please bring some Thirst Aid?"

"The ignorance of that doll!" Vanessa said. "I've explained to her that it's FIRST Aid, what you do before the doctor comes, like bandaging our throats (Jane and I put on the Red Cross things to do it in), but she will pretend she thinks it's Thirst Aid! It's because they rhyme, you know," she whispered, "she can't remember the difference."

"It isn't," said Lupin, who agreed with

Amanda. "It's because it's the same as lemonade and orangeade, so it *must* be Thirst Aid, mustn't it, Mrs. Small? And our throats are so sore, we are very thirsty," she croaked.

Elizabeth laughed at them again. No wonder their throats were sore, with all this croaking. She was afraid they would expect ice-cream, too.

"Wait a minute," she said, "I've got just the thing, as Vanessa would say."

"I don't know whether I would until I see it," remarked Vanessa.

But Elizabeth was half-way downstairs. She ran over to the lorry, and with a struggle managed to unload the orangeade. She rolled it to the door. In the garden was Jacqueline, smiling and looking sly.

"Help me upstairs with this," Elizabeth said.

The paying-guest did so, and then disappeared again. She did not want to go to bed. Elizabeth rolled the bottle in.

"Whatever is it?" said all the dolls together.

"Thirst Aid," said Elizabeth. And she fetched cups and gave them some.

"It's orangeade!"

"Yes."

"It's *lovely*," said Lupin.

"What an immense quantity," said Vanessa, sipping. "Enough for a hospital."

"She means what a lot," whispered Jane to Lupin.

"Now," Elizabeth said, "it's a good idea, and I'll be the surgeon myself, as I know all about it."

"Hooray," shouted Amanda, out loud, forgetting her throat.

"You don't need your tonsils out, that's clear," said Vanessa in a spiteful whisper, "so get up and help Mrs. Small."

"Shan't," said Amanda in a croak.

"I must have someone to help with the stretcher. . . ." Elizabeth said.

"Stretcher?" said Vanessa. "Who are you going to stretch, pray? I dare say Lupin could be a bit longer, but I am the size I like."

Lupin looked alarmed, but Elizabeth said quickly:

"It's all right, it's to carry you on, Lupin, when you're asleep. I know, I'll get the monkey."

All the dolls shrieked aloud, and then suddenly stopped and coughed.

"I can walk in my sleep," said Jane.

"It wouldn't be good for you, after an operation," Elizabeth explained. "Now, settle down and keep still, while I get things ready. The bathroom can be the operating-theatre."

"Theatre! Mrs. Small," whispered Vanessa, sternly after her. "A theatre is not where you take out people's sore throats. It is where you act a play."

"That's just what I'm going to do," Elizabeth said. "I'm not going to cut you up properly, it might kill you."

Jane looked relieved, and Elizabeth ran down the stairs and out of the back door.

"Monkey!" she called. "Come and help me with this stretcher!" And she ran over the lawn and fetched the deck chair.

The monkey came down by the fire-escape, looking very pleased.

"We may as well take her voice right away while we're at it," he said, for he had heard the plan down the chimney.

"Whose?" said Elizabeth.

"Old red cheeks, I gets tired of her voice."

"I expect she gets tired of yours, too. We shall need your bodkin."

The monkey sometimes wore a bodkin for a sword. He fetched it, and then helped Elizabeth up with the deck chair.

"Bless my soul! Strike me pink!" called the parrot from the dining-room.

"Now," Elizabeth said, going into the ward, "you all have to have a prick to send you to sleep."

"You'd think a prick would wake you up, Mrs. Small," sniffed Vanessa.

Amanda shrieked and hid under the bed-clothes. Lupin said:

"I'm asleep already," and Jane turned pale. Vanessa, seeing the bodkin, lay down quickly and started to snore. As for Robin, he really was asleep.

"But it doesn't hurt a bit, because I rub some magic stuff on your arm first," said the surgeon, "and anyway this bodkin is quite blunt."

She walked round with the bodkin and the jar of cold cream. The bodkin certainly looked big.

"There. It doesn't hurt at all, does it, Jane?"

"No," said Jane, happily, closing her eyes.

The prick worked on everyone except Amanda.

"But it hasn't sent me to sleep at *all*," she said naughtily, winking at the monkey.

"If you don't go to sleep, you can't have the operation, and if you don't have the operation, you won't be able to have any. . . ."

But before this long sentence was finished, Amanda was asleep.

"Come on, Monkey, we'll do Robin first, as he's so good."

Elizabeth and the monkey lifted Robin out of his cradle on to the deck chair. They trotted off towards the door, and out of the corner of her eye Elizabeth saw four heads rise up from four pillows, with half an eye open each.

In the bathroom, they laid the stretcher across the bath, and Elizabeth tied her hand-kerchief round her mouth. Behind her there was a light pattering noise, and she even thought she heard a giggle.

She opened Robin's mouth, fiddled about inside and rubbed on some more cold cream.

"All done," she said, and lifted up her end of the stretcher.

There was a rustle and a whisper and a creaking of beds.

"Quick, they're coming," she heard Amanda say.

"It certainly was quick," said Vanessa's voice. "He can't have had very many tonsils."

But when they reached the ward, there were four mounds in the four beds, though Amanda's and Lupin's were shaking.

"They've been out of bed," said the monkey. "I sees 'em at it."

"Then they can't be asleep, and I can't do them," Elizabeth said loudly.

"Oh, Mrs. Small," came a muffled groan from beneath the bedclothes.

"Me next, me next!" said Amanda, looking out.

Vanessa's feather appeared:

"You're not a patient at all," she snapped, "you're an im-patient. Be quick, all the same, Mrs. Small," she ordered, "and get us all done, because I'm sick of being in bed, and it's bad for my feather!"

"All she wants is the ice-cream," said the monkey. "Who's next?"

Lupin rode on the stretcher with her legs in the air, Amanda bounced all the way, and Vanessa went on talking even when her tonsils were being taken out. Only Jane closed her eyes, lay still and behaved as she should.

"Now," said Elizabeth, when it was all over, "they won't come round for some time, so you can come and help me with the groceries, Monkey."

"Who won't come round?" asked Vanessa, sitting up at once. "The neighbours? I should hope not indeed, with us all in bed like this."

"Did you say groceries, Mrs. Small?" said Jane timidly.

"I'm better," said Lupin, bouncing in her bed.

"So am I," yelled Amanda, and she leapt out of bed, and rushed to the window. "Vanessa! Vanessa! There's a huge, red lorry outside!"

All the dolls followed her and peered out over the front garden.

"Oh! What is it?" said Lupin.

"It's full of things!" said Jane.

"There's the paying-guest," said Amanda, who had been watching something moving between the packets.

"Quick! She'll eat the lot!" Vanessa said. "If it's the groceries, as I think I heard you say, dear Mrs. Small, though they've been so long coming I'd quite given them up. All follow me, and we'll take them in!" And she turned and ran down the stairs, the dolls scampering after her. They were tired of tonsils and had forgotten the ice-cream. Elizabeth ran after them. By the time she got there, Amanda had swung herself into the lorry and was punching Jacqueline, who had eaten most of the sugar. Jane had lifted Lupin in; Vanessa was shouting commands to them all and nobody was taking any notice.

"*Do* be careful," Elizabeth begged, "or you'll

spill things. Some of them haven't got any lids!"

"How very careless of the grocer, I shall com-
plain," Vanessa shouted. "Just hand them down
to me and Jane," she went on, her feather jumping with excitement.

"Wait a minute, let me help," said Elizabeth.

But it was too late. Amanda and Lupin had
lifted the lid of treacle on to the edge of the
lorry, and Vanessa and Jane had stretched up to
reach it. Just as they did so the lid tipped and a
great, curling, golden stream of syrup de-
scended on Jane's dark wooden head.

Amanda shrieked with laughter.

"You clumsy doll!" Vanessa stormed.

"Quick, quick, what a waste!" said Lupin,
jumping down and rushing to Jane.

Jane looked very surprised, and opened her
mouth, and stuck out her tongue, and licked the
lovely treacle, smiling.

"Fetch some spoons," Elizabeth said, "and
catch it, before it reaches the ground! What a
good thing it's Jane, she's so smooth."

They all had a race with the treacle. Jacqueline and the monkey did not bother about
spoons, but simply caught it in their hands.
There was a licking, slapping noise as everybody spooned it in.

"Delicious treacle," said Vanessa stickily,

"made all the sweeter by falling over dear Jane. And excellent for our sore throats, no doubt. I hope you're getting your share, Jane? Lick hard, and keep your eyes shut. Splendid," Vanessa went on, nodding. "Must you go, dear Mrs. Small? You can trust us to unpack these groceries, we shan't spill anything else, I promise you. Most generous and genteel of you to arrange them. Come again soon!"

"Look after Robin," Elizabeth said, "and give him some orangeade! And take his temperature!"

"We shall. Good-bye, good-bye! Oh, be careful, Jane!" she said, as Jane waved a treacly arm and smiled.

The rest waved their spoons and hands, and their good-byes were thick and rather stuck together.

The monkey had climbed back to the roof again.

"I 'ope there's more in the well," he called to Elizabeth.

"What well?" she said.

"The treacle well," said the monkey, wisely. And he raised a telescope to his eye and looked at her as she went. It was a piece of macaroni.

III

HAIRDRESSING

WHEN Elizabeth went to call on the dolls again, Edward had taken the red lorry.

As she went to the door, the monkey leaned down over the roof and whispered anxiously:

"It's a good job you've come, Mrs. Small.

That old red cheeks is torturing the paying-guest."

"What!"

"Well, I keeps hearing screams and shrieks from her room."

"She couldn't be," said Elizabeth.

And she knocked at the door and pushed it open.

"Vanessa," she called, "it's me, can I come in?"

Jane leaned over the stairs and gazed at Elizabeth.

"Oh, Mrs. Small, do come up. We're all in Jacqueline's room, as it's next to the bathroom."

"Whatever are you doing?" Elizabeth asked, beginning to climb the stairs. She followed Jane up the two flights to the top floor of the dolls' house. There on Jacqueline's door was a notice, written in Jane's writing:

MADAM VANESSA
HARE DRESSA

"Oh, I see!" said Elizabeth. "What a good idea."

"Yes, some of it is," said Jane, looking doubtful, as a scream from inside made them jump.

She pushed open the door.

"Come in, come in, dear Mrs. Small," Vanessa said, waving a pink comb and a black brush. Elizabeth recognized them both at once. The comb she had bought for the dolls and put on Vanessa's dressing-table. The brush was an eye-brow brush of her mother's which Elizabeth had brought to go with the comb.

"Mrs. Small!" said Lupin, running up. "Vanessa says she's got to wash our hairs too!"

Vanessa went on combing Amanda's fair silky hair, as she sat on a chair by the dressing-table. "Hold still, Amanda," she snapped, as Amanda tugged and screamed. "The fact is, Mrs. Small, their hair hasn't been washed for months, it's a perfect disgrace. Added to which they all got treacle in it, particularly Jane. Now, I go once a fortnight to the hairdresser, as you know. So I thought they would all like it better if I pretended to be a proper hairdresser. But they are most ungrateful. All right, Amanda, we'll try the brush instead." And Vanessa began to brush Amanda's hair with the large brush. "Really, you know, I think it must be meant for the sort of brush that goes with the dust-pan, but it seems quite clean and for Amanda's thick hair, does very well."

"Oh, it's really too big," Elizabeth sighed. "I was afraid so, but the comb's all right."

"Delightful," said Vanessa. "Now, come along Lupin, stop that game."

For Lupin and Jacqueline, tired of waiting, were doing backward somersaults as fast as they could over the end of Jacqueline's bed, and laughing breathlessly. Lupin came slowly towards the hairdresser's chair.

"Now, Jane, bring that cape thing to put round her neck. That's it. Jane's my assistant, Mrs. Small, and very good she is too," said Vanessa as Jane brought a bedspread to put round Lupin. "Now the scissors."

"Vanessa!" said Elizabeth, "you're not going to cut Lupin's hair, are you? It may not grow again!"

Vanessa looked cross.

"Well, Mrs. Small," she said, tugging at Lupin's hair with the pink comb, "it certainly is the most peculiar hair. It's *wool,* like a sheep, you know, or a vest," she said in her loud whisper. "After all, it grows again on a sheep. If I trim it, it may grow better."

"All right, but not much, then," Elizabeth said.

And she took the scissors from Jane and began to cut the ends off Lupin's hair.

Lupin screamed.

"It's those huge shears," Vanessa remarked, "they're enough to make anybody scream. They're meant for cutting hedges, not hair." She sniffed. They were Elizabeth's sewing scissors.

"That's enough," Elizabeth said.

"Very well. Sweep up the pieces, Jane. Oh *no, not* with the hair brush. Whatever will the customers think? The duchess, for instance. She's just telephoned and made an appointment."

"Now what shall we do with Jacqueline's hair?" said Lupin. "Cut Jacqueline's, it's ever so long."

"I don't see why I should do anything to the paying-guest's," Vanessa sniffed. "After all, coming from Paris you'd expect her to have it seen to herself; unless she pays extra," she added hopefully.

"Sit on the chair, Jacqueline," said Elizabeth, "and we'll just comb it."

Jane undid the ribbons from Jacqueline's hair. It was very thick when they had unplaited it.

"Did you ever see such a lot of hair," Vanessa said rather jealously. "When I was a girl, I could sit on mine, of course."

"Go on," said a gruff voice down the chimney. "It's chairs you sit on, not hairs."

"Take no notice, it's that monkey. He knows nothing about it, not having any hair. Only a poor kind of fur."

Elizabeth combed out Jacqueline's hair, more gently than Vanessa, so that she did not scream.

"Come along, now," Vanessa said, leading the way into the bathroom. "Shampooing next. Which brave doll is going first?" And she rolled up her sleeves and knelt by the bath which was steamy with hot water.

"Why does Vanessa——" said Lupin.

"*Madame* Vanessa," put in that lady.

"She keeps on saying shampooing. What is shampooing?" Lupin whispered.

Amanda whisked the water up.

"It's a grand name for soap," Elizabeth said.

"Hush, Mrs. Small," whispered Vanessa, making a face. "Don't mention the word soap. It's shampoo, quite another thing. Doesn't get in your eyes. Unless you keep them open. Which is your fault. Come along, Jane, then, you'll have to lead the way, as everybody is so cowardly."

"No, no," Elizabeth said. "Please don't wash Jane's hair, Vanessa." For Jane was a wooden doll, and her smooth black hair was painted on.

"Why ever not?" Vanessa snapped. "She was simply covered in treacle! Though I admit there was not much left when these greedy dolls had finished."

"Well, because she only needs some good hair oil and a polish——" Elizabeth began.

"She's not a table, Mrs. Small," said Vanessa.

"No, but she's made of the same kind of stuff. And if you wash the paint off, she'll turn into a blonde."

"Gentlemen like blondes best," called the monkey.

"Well, you are *not* a gentleman," answered Vanessa, in the direction of the fireplace.

"What's a blonde?" said Lupin.

"I am," said Amanda proudly, "that's why the monkey likes me best."

"Well, he'd have to like you best as he's your husband."

"But what does it mean?" persisted poor Lupin.

"It means fair-haired," Elizabeth explained. "It's the opposite to a brunette, which is dark-haired, like Vanessa and Jane are."

"Well, after all that," snapped Vanessa, who was tired of kneeling, "are you willing to be a blonde, Jane, or not?"

"No, I'll do Jane while you do Amanda,"
Elizabeth said firmly. And she pushed the
squealing Amanda down by the bath. Vanessa
seized her head and dabbed it into the water.

"It's in my eyes," wailed Amanda.

"Well, keep them shut as I told you," Vanessa
said, rubbing. "Anyway it can't be, because it's
only a sham poo and not a real poo at all, so
don't be ridiculous."

"It's in my ears," yelled Amanda. "I'm deaf."

"It's a pity you're not dumb," Madame Vanessa said.

Elizabeth took some cold cream, rubbed it on
Jane's head, and then polished with the bedspread. She also polished her face.

"You're having a massage," she said.

"Am I? It feels very soothing," said Jane. Her
face shone with pleasure, and the cold cream.

"I'm afraid Amanda's hair has gone a bit
straight," remarked the hairdresser as she dried
it. "Never mind, we'll curl it with the tongs
when it's dry." And she pointed to an odd hair
pin which somebody had dropped in the dolls'
house.

"That's a hair pin," said Elizabeth.

"It's far too big for a hair pin," Jane said.

"It's either a pair of curling-tongs or a cro-
quet hoop, and I don't care which," Vanessa

said crossly. "Come *on*, Lupin, or we'll never get done. All the customers are queuing up."

"There aren't any customers," said Amanda, rubbing her hair.

"Don't get Lupin's head too wet, Vanessa," warned Elizabeth. Lupin was made of stuff.

"You seem to think you know more about hairdressing than I do, Mrs. Small," Vanessa said.

"Well I know what people's heads are made of," said Elizabeth.

"I know what Lupin's is made of," whispered Vanessa, "and that's cotton wool. There you are, Lupin, go to that drier and get it buzzed dry."

Lupin sat under the bedside lamp which was in Jacqueline's room, and Amanda began to buzz. But as she soon got tired of doing it, Lupin had to buzz for herself.

"Now, quickly, paying-guest," Vanessa snapped, "or I shan't do it at all. *Vite!*" she said.

This was a word Jacqueline knew since it meant "quick" in French. So she ran to the bath and knelt down. Vanessa pushed her head in. Jacqueline's long hair floated in the bath like chestnut-coloured seaweed. Vanessa gave it an angry rub. Jacqueline was a china doll and her hair was glued on and the water was hot. Jacqueline's beautiful hair floated right off into the water.

"Oh, I say!" screamed Amanda, "look what Vanessa's done to the paying-guest! Quick, Mrs. Small, do come!"

All the dolls rushed to the bath, to see Jacqueline lift up her bald head.

"Take her hair out quickly and squeeze it dry," Vanessa said. "Perhaps she hasn't noticed, being French."

But poor Jacqueline began to sob.

"Never mind, Jacqueline," Elizabeth said quickly, "it's quite easy to stick it on again, and as soon as I can I will. And after all, lots of people *do* have hair that takes off——"

"Madame Vanessa, for one," called the monkey down the chimney.

Vanessa took no notice.

"You'll just have to wear a ribbon like I do," she said.

But Jacqueline still cried.

Elizabeth squeezed the hair dry and put it on to her head again.

"I know," she said, "you can have a new hair style, to make up. What would you like, a bun?"

"I would, I would," said Lupin.

"What kind of a bun?" she added.

"A currant bun," jeered the monkey.

"She's quite greedy enough without wearing a bun," said Vanessa. "Besides, I was thinking of having one myself, and we can't all be the same."

"A pony's tail!" Elizabeth said, and tied the long, wet hair round with a ribbon at the back.

Jacqueline ran to the mirror. It was all steamed over, and on it was a picture of Vanessa with a mouth like a rat-trap.

"Who drew that?" Vanessa said crossly.

"I did," said Amanda. "It's you."

"It's no such thing," Vanessa said, and she wiped it off viciously with the bedspread. "Anyway, it's gone. Now, Jacqueline."

"*Oui! Oui!*" Jacqueline said, clapping her hands and smiling. She loved to be in the fashion.

"That's all right then," Elizabeth said with relief. "And when I come again, Vanessa, I'll bring something to stick it on with. I must go now."

"Must you, Mrs. Small? We are all going to have tea, while the hairs dry, and you are very welcome to stay."

HAIRDRESSING

"Another time," Elizabeth called out from the stairs. "Don't come down. You'll all catch chills!"

"Very well, dear Mrs. Small. Good-bye! Come again soon!"

"Good-bye!" called the others. "Good-bye."

"Don't think much of that for a hairdresser's," said the monkey, as she walked away. "No dyeing. Why, they could have made some of them ginger." The monkey was ginger himself.

"Vanessa would think dyeing was vulgar, I'm sure."

"I died once," the monkey said, looking puzzled, for he had once pretended to be dead.

"That's another kind of dying altogether," said Elizabeth as she waved at him.

IV

THE BAND

ELIZABETH went up the dolls' house path one day pushing a little jar of glue in front of her. She was going to stick on Jacqueline's hair. But as she got near the front door, such a loud, wild noise started up from somewhere that she nearly jumped out of her skin.

"Oh," she said, half aloud, "whatever is that?"

It was a clanging, banging, tapping, trumpeting, whistling noise: and yet, there seemed to be a rhythm to it, and Elizabeth almost thought she could recognize a tune.

She stepped back and looked up at the roof. As she did so the monkey came into view. He danced up to the edge of the roof, lifting his big feet solemnly, bending his body backwards and forwards, and nodding his head at Elizabeth. But he said nothing and there was a distant look in his eye.

"What are you doing, Monkey?" she called.

But he did not answer. He simply turned round and went rocking and rolling back to the other side of the roof.

"Good gracious," said Elizabeth, and she hurried round the house to find the dolls. The noise from the garden grew deafening. She put her hands over her ears and stood staring with amazement.

In the middle of the lawn was a large, round, brightly coloured thing, like the roundabout in the children's playground, and on this stood Vanessa with a pencil in her hand. She was beating time with the pencil, waving her other hand, and tapping with her toe, and as she did so she screamed:

"One two three, one two three, long live our Gracious Queen, God save the Queen—two three, keep your eyes on the stick, Lupin, you make me sick——"

All the dolls blew, banged, tapped or whistled, but they were far too busy to look at the conductor, and none of them saw Elizabeth. But Vanessa did. She waved her free hand wildly at Elizabeth and sang:

"Here comes dears Mrs. Small
God save us all!"

"Mrs. Small! Hooray!" yelled Amanda running up to her and clapping two saucepan lids in her face. "We've got a lovely band, and you're just in time!"

"We needed another," said Jane, dancing over the lawn with the hammer of the toy xylophone.

"The more the merrier, dear landlady," called Vanessa from her platform. "And the more the noisier too."

"Come on, come on," Lupin said. "What will you play? We're very good!"

"They're NOT very good at all," Vanessa said. "Why, Mrs. Small had to put her hands over her ears, I saw her." The dolls looked crestfallen. "All the same, we hope we may get better. The fact is, Mrs. Small, we found this bandstand in the garden, and it seemed a pity not to use it, so we all found things to play, and we're having a practice. I thought it was time I did something to teach them some music and rhythm, because you know, the piano needs tuning," she whispered behind her hand, "and. . . ."

"It doesn't play at all, however hard we thump," Amanda said.

"No piano likes to be thumped," Vanessa remarked, "so I don't wonder it doesn't play. And when the bandstand came———" she broke off.

"Bandstand?" Elizabeth said. "I don't think it could be." She looked at it, puzzled: she thought she had seen it before, somewhere. "Anyway," she said quickly as she saw Vanessa toss her feather, "it does very well for one. Let's go on."

"Band, take your places," Vanessa commanded, tapping the pencil on the bandstand.

"It's a skiffle group," jeered the monkey, who

was sitting on the roof, looking quite tired. "I tried to teach 'em how to rock an' roll, but they're behind the times. It's a jazz band, if it's anything."

"Take no notice," Vanessa ordered. "But I do think, Mrs. Small, if that monkey is to be allowed to rock and roll on our roof, that you should put the rent *down*. Not up."

"I wasn't going to put it up," Elizabeth began. "I know, I'll fetch the comb," she went on, and she ran into the house.

"Comb?" Vanessa shrieked.

"Yes, I can play on it!"

"Bless my soul. I never heard of anyone playing on a comb, or a brush for that matter," said the conductor of the band, tapping her toe. "Come along, paying-guest, get ready with that drum."

Jacqueline smiled. In one hand she had a red trumpet, as big as herself, and in the other a spoon. She sat next to the dolls' house pail, turned upside down on the lawn, ready to drum on it with the spoon. Elizabeth ran out with the small pink comb and a piece of paper.

"You do this," she said, and sang a tune on it.

"What a buzzy noise," Lupin said. "You

sound like a bee." She herself had the little cow bell, which Vanessa used to ring when she wanted to make the dolls come, and one of Edward's wooden bricks, which she tapped with a fork.

"Listen, Mrs. Small!" Jane said, playing quite a pretty tune on the xylophone.

"Good, Jane," Vanessa said, "but nobody asked you to play a solo that I know of."

Jane blushed, and stopped at once. She was a modest doll, unlike Amanda, who blew a shrill blast on the little yellow whistle which she had in her mouth all the time.

"Very bad for her," Vanessa remarked, "and looks as if she's smoking a cigar, but at least it stops her talking and she has both hands for the cymbals."

Amanda giggled and grunted, and the whistle made little jerky shrieks.

"Now come along, for goodness sake," Vanessa went on. "We've wasted enough of our precious practice time. Mrs. Small, you shall choose the next tune. I must say the National Anthem was not very successful. You would expect them to know that, but they're all so ignorant. . . ." She finished in a whisper, nodding at Elizabeth.

"She doesn't know it herself," called the monkey, "those words was all wrong."

"How does he know, pray?" Vanessa said, blushing, "He's certainly not English, because monkeys don't grow in England, so that's that. What is it to be, Mrs. Small?"

"Humpty Dumpty!" yelled Lupin.

"Hush-a-bye baby," suggested Jane, for even she was excited.

"Frère Jacques!" screamed Jacqueline.

"That's about her brother, of course," Vanessa sniffed, "and it's too French for the rest of us, and anyway, I said Mrs. Small." And she stamped her foot.

Amanda blew another long blast on her whistle. The black velvet kitten, wandering out of the kitchen door, heard this, and rushed up to Amanda, and rubbed against her, and squeaked, and clambered on her knee.

"He loves the whistle, the higher the better," Jane explained. "He's a very musical kitten."

"He ought to have a fiddle, of course," Vanessa said, "but we haven't one, though I dare say if I looked in the loft I might find one."

"I didn't know there was a loft," Elizabeth said.

"What's a loft?" asked Lupin.

"I'm aloft," called the monkey.

"Will you choose a tune or won't you?" Vanessa snapped, pointing her stick at Elizabeth and waggling it.

"I've been trying to think of an easy one," Elizabeth said hastily. Vanessa looked offended at this.

"We can play most things," she said in a huffy voice.

"Three Blind Mice," Elizabeth said. "Does everybody know it?"

"They're NOT blind, not our mice," said Lupin.

"If you mean the creatures in the stable, they're horses, anyway," Vanessa said.

"We need a carving knife to cut off their tails with," said Amanda.

"No" wailed Lupin. "You shan't cut off their tails!"

"It's only in the song, Lupin," Elizabeth explained, "it's not true, anyway."

"WILL you all stop talking, and begin," Vanessa yelled, getting angry, and holding her stick in the air. "One, two, three, four!"

"It *can't* be four if it's *three* mice," Lupin argued. But this was drowned in noise, as all the dolls, led by Elizabeth, started shakily upon

the tune. Amanda clashed her saucepan lids out
of time, and could only whistle on one note;
Jacqueline beat her drum to a quite different
time, as she did not know the tune at all, and
blew the trumpet, also on one note, but a lower
one; Lupin rang her bell whenever she thought
she would, and forgot to tap her box much;
Jane's tinkly notes were completely drowned
by the others, and Elizabeth buzzed so loudly
that the comb tickled her lips and made her
laugh. When they got to the fast part, Vanessa's
stick beat more and more wildly.

"Faster, faster," she yelled, stamping her
wooden toe.

The fastness went to everybody's head. Lupin tapped Jane instead of her box, and as
Jane's head was wooden it sounded very nice;
Jacqueline banged her spoon on Amanda.
Amanda clashed her saucepan lids at Elizabeth,
and blew her whistle so loudly that she fell over
backwards; Elizabeth hummed herself out of
breath, Jane ran the hammer up and down the
xylophone faster and faster like someone run-
ing up and down stairs: and the monkey
rocked and rolled himself right off the roof and
landed on the lawn.

"It serves-him-right," sang Vanessa to the last

line of the song, and shut her mouth like a
trap.

"Come along, again," she said quickly, "while
we can still remember it."

"Again, again," yelled Lupin.

They did it several times, and each time was
louder than the one before. At last Elizabeth
was laughing so much that she could blow no
longer.

"The trouble is," she panted, 'nobody' would
know it was Three Blind Mice."

"We know, and we're the only people that
matter," Amanda said.

"It sounds very modern," said Jane.

"I can't hear it when I'm doing it," said Lupin.

"It would be quite all right," Vanessa said,
"if you would only watch me, and all play the
same thing. More tune, that is what we need."

"What we needs," said the monkey, who had
picked himself up and was walking round Vanessa's circular platform, "is a hurdy-gurdy, they
plays tunes."

"He means a barrel-organ. He used to live on
one," Elizabeth said.

"That's just where he would live, and it's a
pity he doesn't live there still," Vanessa snapped.
"What are you doing, you make me dizzy, go

back on your roof!" she said, as he walked round and round.

A metal rod came up from the centre of the bandstand, and was bent over towards the edge. At the end was a wooden knob. The third time the monkey got to this, he stopped, and reached forward and took hold of the knob.

"Strike me pink," he said.

"One of these days," said Vanessa, "I *shall* strike you, pink or not."

"It's a handle," the monkey said, "and handles is meant for turning. What's the use of a handle unless you turns it?" And he began to walk round again, pushing the handle with his big paw.

The most delightful tune tinkled into the garden as the monkey turned the handle.

"Listen!" screamed Lupin, and she stopped pricking Amanda with her fork.

"Oh, how lovely!" said Jane, clasping her hands.

"*Ciel!*" exclaimed Jacqueline.

"Bless my soul," said Vanessa, "how very genteel to be sure," and she folded her arms and nodded her head in time with the music. "What a very surprising bandstand, no need for a band at all."

"It's a wireless," little Lupin said.

"Or a gramophone," added Amanda.

"Hush, do listen," said Jane. "Oh, how pretty."

The monkey began to walk faster.

"Oh, look out Vanessa!" yelled Elizabeth, seeing what would happen. For the handle of her musical-box (she had just realized what it was) was coming nearer and nearer to Vanessa who still stood on top.

"I *am* looking out," Vanessa said crossly, gazing over the lawn; when SWISH! The handle pushed against her and swept her off, and she flew through the air and landed on her feather upon the velvet lawn. The monkey ran faster and faster, giggling to himself. Jane rushed to Vanessa. The tune spun and tinkled.

"Oh, poor Vanessa," she said.

"Hush!" Vanessa whispered, scrambling up, putting her hat straight, and holding her finger in the air. "Not hurt at all, no need to make a fuss. Just listen!" Vanessa always made the best of things.

Faster and faster tinkled the tune, until the monkey flopped, dizzy, on the lawn.

"Let me, let me," Amanda said.

"Me!" wailed Lupin.

"You can't reach," said Amanda, seizing the handle.

"Don't quarrel, you shall all turn in turn," commanded Vanessa: and looked very puzzled at what she had said.

"It's prettier than the band, but not so much fun," announced Amanda, "and I'm so dizzy, the house is going round and round!"

Everybody turned and looked at the house.

"It's not," said Lupin staring at it.

"It is, it's falling right over!" screamed Amanda.

"It's you that's falling over," said the monkey, pushing her.

Amanda lay and giggled on the lawn.

"When you get dizzy you can turn it the other way," Elizabeth told Jane.

"It might break the tune," Jane said anxiously.

"No, it won't, it plays both ways."

"How very clever and good-natured of it," Vanessa said. "A remarkable bandstand."

"It's a musical-box, Vanessa," said Elizabeth.

"Too big," said Vanessa, firmly.

"Well, anyway, I enjoyed the band," said Elizabeth truthfully, "and now I must go."

"So did I, Mrs. Small," said Vanessa, "and

it's very good for young people to make a noise sometimes."

"Red cheeks is over a hundred," remarked the monkey, "so it must be good for old people too."

Vanessa blushed.

"Well, he's so old, he can't even remember," she snapped. "Must you go, Mrs. Small? Thank you for coming and we'll expect you soon, and I hope this musical bandstand will still be here, but you can never tell in this house, things come and they go."

"Good-bye, good-bye!" yelled the dolls.

They all waved, but their eyes were on the musical-box. Elizabeth left them turning its handle and dancing round it, enchanted with the sparkling tune.

The monkey was on the roof again, holding out his cocked hat hopefully, for pennies.

V

JANE THE POETESS

ELIZABETH thought it was a pity that Jane, who seemed to be so fond of writing notices and things, should have to write with a matchstick dipped in paint, which she called her pen. What could she give her for a real pen? She felt sure that Jane and Vanessa, being rather old-fashioned dolls, would like a quill pen better than, perhaps, a mapping pen. She found a small white goose feather and got somebody to sharpen it so that it would write. Jane's ink pot should be a tiny, tiny glass bottle which Elizabeth's mother had bath essence in. When it was empty, Elizabeth filled it with ink from her bottle. Then she took the quill and ink to the dolls' house door and knocked. Everybody came to the door.

"Good evening, Mrs. Small," said Vanessa.

"It's good morning, really," Elizabeth said, surprised.

"Well, we must have a change sometimes," Vanessa explained.

"Look, Jane," said Elizabeth, "I've brought you a pen and ink, so that you can write properly."

"How very delightful to be sure," Vanessa said, her feather bobbing. "We'll be able to write letters! At least, Jane will, I haven't time myself," she coughed.

"She can't write," said a voice from the roof.

Vanessa slammed the door.

As for Jane, she was gazing at the little pen and the glass ink pot, quite speechless and very pink.

"Oh, Mrs. Small," she said. "Thank you.

Now I shall be able to write down all my poems!"

"You see," Vanessa said, "you couldn't have brought Jane a better present. She has always wanted to be a poetess."

"What's a poetess?"

"A lady who writes poems, Lupin, and a very clever and splendid thing to be," Vanessa explained.

"Oh, Jane!"

"When will you begin?"

"Where *are* all your poems?"

"In my heart," said Jane, "wanting to come out."

"Let's make a little book, like you once made for the bazaar," suggested Elizabeth.

"The very thing," said Vanessa.

They ran upstairs, all excited about Jane the poetess. Elizabeth found a sheet of paper, and they folded it, and slit the edges and made a little book with a lot of leaves.

"Now, a piece of silk to tie them together in a bow," Vanessa said.

"Jane can write at the parlour table, can't she?" said Lupin.

"Certainly. Bring the quill and ink up."

"Doesn't the ink *smell* lovely?" said Amanda, smelling the bottle.

The bath essence, thought Elizabeth, must be very strong.

"Now, my dear Jane, we shan't disturb you —much," Vanessa said, as Jane settled herself at the parlour table. It had a pattern of flowers painted upon it and was very suitable for writing poems at.

"Hadn't we better leave her alone?" Elizabeth said.

"I want to see that feather write," said Lupin.

"I want to see Jane think," added Amanda.

"You can't see anyone think," said Vanessa.

But Elizabeth was not so sure.

Jane dipped the quill in the ink.

"That's the wrong end!" Lupin cried.

"Nonsense, Lupin, you know nothing about it," said Vanessa.

The first thing that happened was a large blot.

"Is that a poem?" said Lupin.

"No, it's a blot," Elizabeth told her.

"It's a plot," said a hollow voice down the chimney.

"Oh, dear," said Jane, "you all make me nervous."

It was no wonder, for Lupin was leaning on her knee, and Amanda on the table, and Vanessa looking over her shoulder tickling her with her feather, and Jacqueline and Elizabeth breathing down her neck. The kitten was making a noise with a marble he had found.

"Get the kitten's pen-wiper," Vanessa said. For the black velvet kitten slept on a flannel pen-wiper.

"That's it. Oh, careful. An even bigger blot."

"What a lovely pattern," Lupin said.

"Just waste that page," Elizabeth said, pulling it out. "Now, everybody, go away and leave Jane in peace," she ordered.

For poor Jane was nearly crying.

"Thank you, Mrs. Small," she said.

Elizabeth pushed the dolls out.

"Now you can get on, Jane."

Jane nodded. She was already busy writing. Elizabeth closed the door.

She went to find Vanessa, who was in her bedroom.

"What I thought, Mrs. Small," she said eagerly, giving Robin's cradle a hasty rock as she passed it, "was that when Jane has finished, she can give a reading, and we can all go to it. That's what real poetesses do, you know, sometimes."

"What a good idea, Vanessa. Will she be shy?"

"Not if I tell her how to do it," Vanessa said.

"I'll go and see how she's getting on," said
Elizabeth.

She peeped in at the parlour door. Jane sat
writing and writing, looking very pink. She
seemed to be half-way through the book already. She did not hear Elizabeth.

"She's nearly finished," Elizabeth reported.

"Splendid! What talent she has. Fancy having so many poems ready at once."

"She said they were all in her heart."

At last, Jane had finished. Elizabeth crept in,
and there was the little book with every page
covered with tiny, tiny writing. Some poems
were long, and some were short, some had long
lines, some had short lines. They were beauti-
fully written, and decorated with curly lines
and squiggles.

"Jane!"

Elizabeth peered. For half a moment she
thought it was all scribble. But, no, she could
just read the words.

"Now, my dear poetess," Vanessa said, sailing
in, "I know you'll be willing to give a reading of
your works and here we all are to listen." And
she began to arrange the parlour chairs in front
of Jane's table. Lupin and Amanda came in and
helped. Jacqueline arrived in her best dress.

"Let's get the parrot," said Lupin, "he'll like it."

And they ran down to the dining-room and staggered upstairs with his cage, Elizabeth helping.

"We ought to charge to come in," Amanda said.

"Children 'alf price," said the parrot at once.

"Isn't he *clever*, Mrs. Small? He must understand what we say."

"Not 'alf, not 'alf, not 'alf price," said the parrot, getting muddled up.

But Jane was watching all these preparations, looking rather unhappy.

"Vanessa, couldn't you read them to yourself?" she said.

Vanessa coughed. "I've got a sore throat," said she firmly. "It's since I had my tonsils out, they weren't very well done."

"You needn't read them aloud," said Jane.

"How can I read them if I don't know what they say?" Vanessa snapped. "Come along, Jane, don't be shy. You're not a coconut. Don't cough, don't stutter, don't splutter, and don't mumble——"

"And don't grumble and don't flutter," sang Amanda, who loved things that rhymed.

"And, above all, don't blush," Vanessa said. "You must lift your head up. You ought to wear a turban, really; lady poets do."

"She's not an Arab or a Turk," said Elizabeth.

"Or a turkey," said Lupin.

Jane giggled.

"If I lift my head up, I can't see the words."

"Then lift the book up. Anyway you know the words."

So everybody settled down, and Jane began. As she read, she grew less shy. As people clapped, she became more pleased and less worried.

There was the one about the monkey falling off the roof, which everybody knew already and joined in. Then there was:

> "Look at the spider on the wall
> Ladies and gentlemen that is all."

Jane pointed as she said it and everybody turned to look. But there was no spider on the wall, only a beautiful one drawn on Jane's page.

"Oh, I like that one," said Lupin, clapping. And there was:

> "A white goose feather
> Is my quill
> And I write my poems
> With a will."

Everybody clapped hard. And Jane read:

"The sun is hot
But I am not
My feet are cold
And I am very old."

Vanessa dabbed her eyes. "Most pathetic," she said. "Reminds me of my dear father, the Duke. Cranberry Castle is always cold in winter, it's too big."

And then there was a poem called "Cooking," which went:

"Amanda chops
And Lupin stirs
Jacqueline tastes
Vanessa bastes
And by the grate
The black cat
Purrs, purrs, purrs."

"Very good!" said all the dolls together, for they liked cooking.

"It ought to be the black cate," Lupin said.

"You've made up 'bastes,'" said Amanda.

"Shush!" said Vanessa. "All poems are made up."

"It's a real word," said Elizabeth.

"Audience, *don't* whisper," Vanessa said.

And there was a poem about the rocking-chair and another about the snow. And there was one about driving in the mouse-and-trap. And a lullaby for Robin. And there was:

"Vanessa has a four poster
Four poster bed
It has curtains at the foot end
And curtains at the head
And if you draw the curtains round
You cannot hear the smallest sound
In the four poster
Four poster bed."

There was a storm of clapping at this one.

"Though it's not quite true," Vanessa said, "but what poem is?"

"*Encore! Encore!*" shouted Jacqueline.

"She means try again," said Vanessa.

And then Jane came to the end of the book and read the last poem, which was about washing day.

"And that's all," she said, smiling.

The whole audience stood up and clapped and cheered, and Lupin and Amanda ran forward and patted the poetess on the back until she choked.

"I always said Jane was very clever," Vanessa

announced, "and I was certainly right. The next question is, where do we keep the book?"

"In the bookshelf," said Amanda.

There was a little bookshelf in the parlour, it was true.

"Unfortunately, there isn't room, as it is full of books, and they won't come out," Vanessa whispered. "We think Amanda must have made them so sticky with jam that they're stuck in forever."

"They came stuck in," said a voice down the chimney.

"What does he know about books?" Vanessa went on crossly. "Nothing at all."

Elizabeth was afraid it was true about the bookshelf: the little books were not real, and would not come out.

"We'll have to get another bookshelf," she said. "Especially if Jane's going to write books often."

"Are you, Jane?" Lupin said.

"Will you write a story, Jane?" Amanda begged.

"Please, please," said Jacqueline. It was one of the words she knew, though she did not know many.

"I might," Jane said.

"Quickly, before the ink's all gone!" said Lupin.

She had taken the quill, and was playing the blot game with a piece of paper left over from making the book, which she folded. The blots ran into patterns.

"The ink won't go on its own," said Vanessa, who had not noticed this. "You ridiculous doll."

"It'll go if Lupin does that," said Jane anxiously.

"I'll bring some more next time I come," Elizabeth promised.

"Look at Lupin!" Amanda said. "Let *me* have a go!"

"Why, what a delightful game," said Vanessa. "Just look, Mrs. Small! Lovely patterns, and no trouble at all! We might have done it when we had the new wallpaper."

Elizabeth was doubtful about this. All the dolls began to do blot patterns in turn upon scraps of paper. Even Jane, who was worried about the ink, could not help having a turn.

"Good-bye!" Elizabeth called. "I think Jane's poems are lovely!"

"Yes, aren't they," Vanessa said, happily. "Look, the image of that monkey!"

"I think my blots are lovely," added Lupin.

"Look at this one! It's a tree, with a leopard under it!"

"Good-bye, Mrs. Small, I'm going to be a blottess!" Amanda called, as Elizabeth went downstairs.

"The only ink what's any fun," said the monkey jealously as Elizabeth walked away, "is invisible ink. Then people can't read what it says."

And he winked at Elizabeth as if he were a spy.

VI

A VISIT TO THE ZOO

W HEN Elizabeth next went to see the dolls
it was a fine spring day which made her want to
go on expeditions. The monkey looked at her
as she came up the path.

"Old red cheeks is dying at last," he announced with gloom.

"Dying!" said Elizabeth. Vanessa could not possibly die, she was sure.

"Sounds like it. I hears what they say. She won't come out of her room, and she won't go to bed. All she does is sits in her chair, the rocking one."

A scuffling, sliding and thumping echoed from the hall, as Elizabeth stood near the front door. Then there was a burst of laughter. It sounded like Amanda's and Lupin's laughter.

"She can't be," Elizabeth said, firmly, "or they wouldn't be laughing." And she listened again.

"If only someone would come to the door," she heard Lupin say.

"Just when we've found this good way to open it," grumbled Amanda. "You'd think they would."

"*You* go to the door," urged Lupin.

"No, I want to open it, I thought of it."

"Let's make the paying-guest go. Where is she?"

"She said it would tear her frills so she wouldn't play."

"My turn, hurry!"

Elizabeth knocked firmly at the door.

"Hooray!" yelled Lupin's voice, and there

was a swish, a thump, a slide and the door flew
open.

"Mrs. Small, Mrs. Small," they both said together, tugging her inside, "we've found the
most lovely way to open the door, and we were
just wanting someone to come——"

"You slide down the bannisters, leap-frog on
to the mat, and the mat takes you to the front
door, and then you open it!" said Amanda. "Go
out again, and I'll do it, go on! We've got very
good, practising."

Elizabeth did as she was told, and this time
Amanda opened the door.

"We'll never do it any other way, it's so easy!"
she said.

"It's not easier than just opening it," Elizabeth said laughing.

"It *is*," they said together, in loud voices.

"Fancy Vanessa letting you."

The two youngest dolls looked at each other,
furtively.

"We don't know what's the matter with Vanessa," Lupin whispered.

"We all wanted to go out, because the monkey's seen a Zoo from the roof, and we asked
Vanessa, and she says she can't come, and that
we're not to go without her, and so we had to do

something, and that's why we did sliding down the bannisters," Amanda explained breathlessly.

"But is she ill?" said Elizabeth, feeling worried.

"She doesn't look ill, she just looks cross as usual."

"She keeps on rocking in her chair."

"Perhaps she's made herself feel sick," Elizabeth suggested. She had done this once herself.

"She won't have us in there, only Jane."

"Where's Jacqueline?"

"She's in her room, because of her frills, we think. Jane stuck her hair on with that glue."

Elizabeth ran up the stairs, and knocked gently at the door of the best bedroom.

"It's me. Mrs. Small," she said.

Jane pattered to the door and opened it.

"Oh Mrs. Small, I'm so relieved to see you," she whispered, "because I'm afraid Vanessa doesn't feel well——"

"I feel perfectly well," roared Vanessa loudly. "I told Jane so."

Elizabeth looked at her, and she glared and began to rock herself again.

"Why shouldn't I stay in my chair, if I want to? And have my meals on a tray? Which Jane kindly arranged."

"No reason, Vanessa, but usually you're always doing things——" Elizabeth began.

"Well, now I'm having a rest, which at my age is only right, such a lady as I was brought up too," she said defiantly. "Go and get me a cup of tea, Jane," she said, and as Jane hurried out closing the door, Elizabeth saw Vanessa's lip tremble.

"I only sent her to get rid of her," she went on, as a tear rolled down her cheek, "I don't know what's the matter, dear Mrs. Small, but I sat down this morning next to Robin, and I can't get up," she sobbed. "I keep rocking to try, but I can't move, my legs won't work, I'm stuck, or paralysed, or whatever they call it! I thought it would alarm everybody, so I pretended I liked it, but I don't, I don't," she finished. "I want to get up and go to the Zoo!"

"Oh, poor Vanessa," Elizabeth said, comforting her. "I'm sure I'll be able to think of something, don't worry. You can't be ill, you look quite all right. Can you sit forward so that I can get my arms under yours and push you?"

"No, that's just it, I can't," Vanessa snapped. "Even my back is stuck. I've grown into the chair," she said.

Elizabeth put her fingers behind Vanessa.

There was a strong smell, and the chair felt sticky.

"Vanessa!" she said, half-laughing. "It's all right, it's glue!"

"GLUE!" shrieked Vanessa.

"Yes, somebody's spilt glue on it, that's all. Wait while I get my scissors, I can cut you out——"

"I won't be cut out!" Vanessa said, for she was very upset. "I'm not cardboard!"

"It's all right, it won't hurt, you wait," and Elizabeth went out. Looking over the bannisters from the top floor was the paying-guest, laughing.

"Jacqueline!" said Elizabeth. "I believe you did it."

The paying-guest nodded.

"*Oui, oui,*" she giggled. "But if you not tell her she not know."

Elizabeth was afraid it served Vanessa right, for she was often unkind to Jacqueline. She fetched the scissors. When she got back, Vanessa looked more cheerful.

"I'll have to cut your dress, Vanessa, but we can make you another."

"It doesn't matter in the least, I have dozens of dresses, and anyway I can wear my tea-gown," Vanessa said airily.

Elizabeth cut the back of Vanessa's dress.

"Now, if I pull your hands, the rest may come off."

"All I care is that I shall come off," Vanessa said, and she gave Elizabeth her little wooden hands, and Elizabeth tugged and Vanessa strained, and there was a loud tearing noise, and Vanessa stood up, with dress in front and petticoat behind.

She danced joyfully round the room.

"Splendid, Mrs. Small, capital, as my father would say (though I never knew what he meant because a capital's a town, you know, or else a letter). What a very great mercy, now my tea-gown and we can all go to this Zoo, or whatever it is that ridiculous monkey has seen through his macaroni. For that's what it is, Mrs. Small, it's not a telescope at all, whatever he says, and everytime I see it it's shorter, which simply means he is nibbling it."

"Vanessa!" said Jane rushing in. And she put down the tea, and hugged Vanessa, almost crying.

"There, there," said Vanessa who was quite herself again. "Though why you're crying, Jane, I don't know, it's I who should have been crying. Which I haven't," she added hastily, winking at Elizabeth, and dabbing her eyes.

"Vanessa, are you better?" said Amanda and Lupin rushing in.

"You see, they're really quite fond of me, though you wouldn't think it," Vanessa said. "I have never been worser, so I can't be better," she went on, getting muddled. "Anyway, I'm quite all right, some stupid person had spilt glue on the chair——"

"I know who that could be," Amanda said.

"Hush," said Elizabeth. "Let's go to this Zoo, quickly, or I'll have to go home. Where is it?"

There was a stampede down the stairs and out into the garden.

"Monkey!" called Amanda. "We're ready, we're all coming to the Zoo. Is it still there?"

The monkey lifted his macaroni and gazed out to the far corner of the nursery.

"Yep," he reported.

"Can we walk?" Vanessa asked.

"I should try, if I was you," the monkey said, solemnly.

"Ridiculous animal," Vanessa snorted, but she was too glad at being free to be cross. "Is it within walking distance?"

He nodded. He swung down from the roof, and they set off. Elizabeth had suddenly realized what the monkey had seen: Edward's Noah's ark. She was afraid the dolls might be a little disappointed at the animals being wooden . . . so she said:

"It's not a Zoo really, at least it's a kind of private Zoo——"

"If it's private we shan't be able to go in," Jane said.

"Yes, we shall, because I know who it belongs to."

"Another of your brothers, no doubt," said Vanessa happily.

"No, the same one, I've only got one."

"Fancy, only one brother, I had seven."

"Where are they all, Vanessa?" said Elizabeth.

"All gone to the wars. They were all soldiers. I haven't seen them for years and years."

They had reached the place where Edward had set out the Noah's ark. He had used the farm fence, and inside it in a long procession were the animals, two by two.

"Bless my soul!" Vanessa said.

"A march past," said the monkey, wisely.

"Past what?" said Lupin.

"They aren't in cages," said Jane, looking nervous.

"They're wooden," cried Amanda.

"Where's the keeper?" Vanessa demanded. "It's most dangerous to have wild animals loose, and I shan't go inside that fence till I know they are harmless."

"They must be harmless, if they're wooden," said Amanda.

"Well, Vanessa's wooden and she's not harmless," whispered the monkey.

"Jane's wooden, and she *is* harmless," replied Elizabeth. "Come on, we'll go in."

"Oh, oh, be careful, they're moving," Lupin said, clutching at Elizabeth.

And they were. As soon as the party got inside the fence, the procession began to move. Led by the elephants, they walked solemnly round in a circle, past the great ark, where Mr. and Mrs. Noah nodded from the steps, the lions, tigers, bears, giraffes, horses, donkeys, zebras, monkeys, camels, yaks, sea-lions, walruses, crocodiles, snakes, to say nothing of the smaller creatures, and the birds.

"I believe they're all tame," Vanessa whispered.

"Yes, I think they are," Elizabeth said, "or they wouldn't be free."

"It's a great thing to be free," said Vanessa, thinking of the glue. "Here, pussy, pussy," she said holding her hand out.

"It's a tiger," Amanda said with scorn.

"A very small one," said Vanessa.

"I love the elephants!" said Lupin. "Do you think I could ride on one?"

"Oh, me too," said Amanda.

"*Moi aussi,*" said Jacqueline, stroking a donkey.

"Look at that creature's neck," Vanessa said, pointing to the giraffe. "Did you ever. That's what comes of always trying to see what you're not meant to see, no doubt. What a lot of scarf he must need."

"What a lot of cough drops, too," said Jane.

Elizabeth followed Lupin and Amanda up to the elephants. They were small, for elephants. ("They must be baby ones," Vanessa remarked.) But they seemed quite gentle. With squeals of joy Lupin and Amanda clambered on their backs: and the two creatures set off round the enclosure.

"Now, Jacqueline, what'll you ride?"

"She'll ride the donkey," Vanessa remarked, "I heard her say so, at least she said 'ass,' which means the same, and anyway it's most suitable to her," she finished venomously.

Jacqueline smiled as Elizabeth helped her on. She did not understand what Vanessa said.

"Jane, would you like a ride?"

Jane looked a little nervous.

"I should *like* one, but——"

"Come along, Jane, it's quite safe," Vanessa said briskly. "Why, look at those two on the elephants! You're not going to be beaten by them, I hope."

"Are *you* going to ride, Vanessa?" said Jane.

"Certainly," said Vanessa, tossing her head. "That is, if anything is big enough to hold me. I really fancy the creature with the neck, then I can hold on to it."

"I'd like the fawn animal with the bulge," Jane said.

So Elizabeth helped them on. The giraffe looked surprised, the camel sneered, but they walked off after the elephants and the donkey. The dolls laughed and waved and called to each other.

"Come on, Mrs. Small, do, it's lovely."

But Elizabeth was watching the monkey. He had found the two Noah's ark monkeys, and they were standing in a huddle, chattering. They were chattering so hard and so fast, it was more like screaming. Nobody could understand what they said.

"Listen to the monkey, Vanessa!"

"It's monkey language," she called. "A waste of time to listen."

They were waving their arms about. The monkey's great flat paws looked like boxing gloves. The two wooden monkeys danced and screamed.

"They're cross, Vanessa!"

"I don't wonder, the monkey often makes me cross. It's a pity we brought him."

"It was his idea," Amanda said.

"Oh, they're fighting!" said Elizabeth.

"It will annoy the keepers," said Jane.

"Stop it at once!" Vanessa yelled from the giraffe. "Or you'll go home!"

"Come on, Monkey!" cheered Amanda, waving him on.

But Lupin looked nervous.

"It may excite the others," Jane said.

The monkeys hit and bit and scratched and punched, all the while chattering and screaming. The dolls' house monkey was bigger than they, but not so hard. At last he seized the thin wooden arm of one of them and held on, yelling. There was a crack, and the arm broke.

"Look what he's done now!"

"Broken his arm!"

"Now that *will* annoy the keepers," Vanessa said, slipping off her giraffe. "All come away, quickly, before we are set on by angry animals!

Come along Jane, Lupin, Amanda! The paying-guest can do as she likes. Leave that monkey to his fate and COME!"

And she skipped for the gate, followed quickly by all the dolls, and Elizabeth. Without looking back, Vanessa pattered off for the dolls' house, holding up her tea-gown, and the rest ran after her.

"Poor Monkey," Amanda panted. "It's two against one, you know."

"It's probably sixty against one by now," Vanessa said with pleasure.

"You are mean, Vanessa."

"Will your brother be cross about the arm?" said Jane, breathlessly.

"Oh, it's only wood," Elizabeth said, "we can stick it on with glue, don't worry."

"Where is that glue?" asked Lupin.

"It was in Jacqueline's room," said Jane, "because I stuck her hair on."

"There—is—none—glue," Jacqueline managed to say.

"Why not, may I ask?" Vanessa demanded. "And you mean 'no glue,' not 'none glue.' And anyway," she said, remembering, "you seem to know a great deal about the glue." And she stared at the paying-guest very hard as they walked up to the front door. Jacqueline giggled.

"Well, I must go," Elizabeth said quickly, to change the subject.

"It was a lovely Zoo!" said Amanda.

"Yes it was," said all the others.

"I loved the elephant ride," Lupin added.

"And at least we've got rid of that monkey," Vanessa said in triumph.

There was a laugh from the roof above them. The monkey had raced home the back way, and was already in his place.

"Hooray!" said the dolls.

"*You* should have stayed in the Zoo," said Vanessa crossly.

"And *you* should have stayed in the glue," croaked the monkey.

VII

THE SWEEP

ELIZABETH mended the ark monkey's arm
with the remains of the glue (there wasn't
much, and no wonder, she thought). She decided she would ask the monkey what they had
quarrelled about. But the next time she visited
the dolls, the roof of the dolls' house seemed to
be empty. If he was there at all he was hiding.

She knocked at the door, but there was no

answer. She put her ear to the letter-box. Noises came from upstairs, Vanessa's voice, and the sound of moving furniture. She peered in at the dining-room window. It looked very strange. The chairs were piled on the table, the side table was pushed to the middle, the rug was rolled up, and the curtains were tied into knots.

"What are they up to now?" she said, and she knocked again. She heard Amanda call:

"We'll have to let him in, Vanessa, or he'll go away, and that would be a waste."

"Very well," said Vanessa's voice, "we're ready downstairs anyway. But he shouldn't come before he says."

"Did he say?" asked Jane.

"Maybe he didn't, but I did," yelled Vanessa's voice.

Elizabeth knocked once more.

"He's getting cross," said Lupin. "Can't I open the door?"

"You are *not* to do that sliding trick!" called Vanessa's voice.

But it was too late, for Lupin had done it, and the door flew open. She shrieked with laughter.

"It's Mrs. Small!" she yelled. "After all."

"Dear, oh dear," Vanessa said, hurrying down

the stairs, her head tied in a duster. "It's not that we're not pleased to see you, dear Mrs. Small——" Vanessa began, irritably.

"Mrs. Small, after all, Mrs. Small, after all," sang Amanda capering about.

"Don't be rude, Amanda——"

"That's not rude," said Elizabeth, "that's a poem."

"Well whatever it is, and poems often can be rude, it's got nothing to do with what I was trying to say, which is that we were expecting the sweep, and we thought you were he, which is why we kept you waiting, because upstairs isn't quite ready——"

"In here is, look," said Jane showing Elizabeth the dining-room.

"Oh, I see," said Elizabeth. "That's why."

"So when he comes he can begin there."

"What have you covered it up with?" Elizabeth asked.

"It's a bedspread," Vanessa whispered, "but it will do for a dust sheet."

"Look at the curtains," said Lupin, proudly, "if you knot them they don't get sooty."

"Come upstairs and help," said Jane.

"Though why we get sooty at all is a mystery," Vanessa went on in a whisper as they trooped up to the parlour, "because, you know, we always have red paper fires, and not coal at all. Clean but cold it is."

"Then why are we having the sweep?" demanded Amanda.

"The sweep suggested it himself. It came on a postcard. And I think it's a very good idea. There may be more soot than we expect. We always had the sweep at Cranberry Castle, and it took days, the boys used to climb about in those great chimneys and get lost, and very black——"

"Just like 'The Water Babies,' " said Elizabeth. Vanessa stared, as she had not read "The Water Babies."

"It's very cruel, Vanessa."

"What's very cruel, sweeping the chimney?"

"No, letting boys climb about up there."

"Oh, I don't suppose this sweep will," Vanessa said airily. "He's very good, at least he says he is. Help me with this carpet, Jane."

They rolled up the carpet. The black velvet kitten rushed inside it.

"Bother this kitten," Vanessa said, "always everywhere."

Lupin and Amanda were covering up the sofa.

"Sheets from our beds," they said, in a whisper. "The paying-guest won't lend hers."

"I don't blame her," Elizabeth said. "They'll get sooty."

Jane covered the parlour clock with Lupin's blue silk romper-suit.

"Now we can't tell the time, we shan't know if he's late or not," Amanda said.

"You can't tell the time anyway," replied Vanessa.

"Neither can she," said a voice down the chimney.

"What I wish," said Vanessa, blushing, "is that the sweep would sweep that monkey off."

There was a hollow laugh from above.

They pushed the parlour table, painted with flowers, up to the piano, and covered them with more pieces from the scrap-box.

"Mustn't get soot in the works," Vanessa said.

"It doesn't work anyway," said Lupin.

But Vanessa always stood up for the piano.

"It's probably old and tired," she whispered.

Amanda stood on the sofa and tied knots in the curtains.

"Well, now we ARE ready," Vanessa said, "so I hope he'll come and not keep us waiting. We don't want the house upside down for ever."

"We don't want the house upside down at all,

Vanessa," said Lupin looking anxious.

"Ridiculous doll. So simple, she is, Mrs. Small, you'd hardly believe it. I mean of course, the things *in* the house, Lupin, being upside down."

"But they're not upside down," Lupin persisted to herself, looking at the piano with wonder.

"If the house were upside down," Amanda began, interested, "would we have to walk on our heads, Vanessa?"

"Certainly not," Vanessa snapped.

"I can't, anyway," said Jane.

"I can," said Amanda, standing on her head.

"So can I," said Lupin, doing likewise and falling over.

"Well, you won't have to, so come down and stop being unladylike——"

There was a loud knock at the door.

"The sweep!" they all yelled, and ran down the stairs.

But Vanessa had the start and she arrived first. She threw open the door, about to say "Come in": and then stared.

The sweep was dressed entirely in black. He had a long, flowing black robe, and a black scarf tied around his head and mouth, so that only his eyes showed. His cheeks, round the eyes,

were black too, perhaps with soot. Amanda
laughed, Lupin clutched Jane, Elizabeth stared,
Jacqueline, who had come silently downstairs,
whispered something in French, and Vanessa
said firmly:

"There is no funeral here. You've come to the
wrong house."

"He's the sweep, Vanessa," Jane said.

"Then why doesn't he say so?"

"I shouldn't think he can say anything," said
Elizabeth.

"How *very* awkward, how are we going to
explain all about it? I've heard of a dumb
waiter, but I've *never* heard of a dumb
sweep——"

"He needn't be deaf as well," said Jane rea-
sonably.

The sweep shook his brushes at Vanessa and
stepped in. Elizabeth looked with interest.
There was an old tooth brush, a paint brush,
and two small wire brushes which her mother
used for cleaning narrow things like teapot
spouts. They had been thrown away, and she
had taken them for the dolls' house. They were
all quite clean, and not sooty, but no one seemed
to notice.

"He appears to be well-armed," Vanessa said.

"Come along in, Sweep," she went on, trying to show him into the dining-room, which was difficult as all the dolls stood in the door. "Out of the way, Amanda."

The sweep poked Amanda with his brush.

"Bless my soul, 'alf price, 'alf price, 'alf price," said the parrot.

"We shall certainly not expect you to do it for half price," Vanessa said graciously, "so pay no attention to that bird."

"He'll get sooty," Lupin said.

"That's his look-out," said Vanessa.

But Lupin covered the parrot's cage with the cover he had at night.

The sweep laid down his brushes, and with dumb show, shooed everybody out of the room.

"But I want to watch," Lupin said.

"You can watch from the garden," said Vanessa. "The first person to see the brush come out of the chimney has won."

"Won what?" said Amanda with excitement.

"The prize," said Vanessa. "Come along, let him get on, now he *is* here. At least he can't waste time gossiping. I suppose all those black things don't show the soot, but he looks more like a monk."

"Or a monkey," Amanda said, and then

stopped, looking puzzled, and secretive.

Vanessa made them all go into the garden.

"We need fresh air, we shall have enough soot when we clear up. All find something to do in the garden."

"How long will he be?" Lupin said, sitting down and gazing at the chimneys, determined to win the prize.

"That depends how long the chimney is," said Vanessa.

"And how long the brushes are, I suppose," said Jane, turning the musical-box.

"I'm going to skate," Amanda said, and Elizabeth followed her to the pond.

"Trust that paying-guest to come out when all the work is done," Vanessa said. "Whenever there is anything to do, she has to go and write to her family, but as soon as we've done it all, down she comes."

Jacqueline smiled and ran to the skating-rink. Lupin grew tired of watching the chimney.

"I'm going to finish my bird-bath," she said.

"Yes, do," said Vanessa.

Elizabeth came to see. Lupin had got one of the lids (the groceries were long since eaten) and had filled it with water and put it near the bird-table. By it she put two pieces of rag, and a little white thing.

"That's the towel, and that's the flannel, and that's the soap," she said.

"Nonsense," Vanessa remarked. "They don't use those. Whoever heard of a bird using soap. They just flutter."

"And splutter," Amanda said, coming back.

"Vanessa, I've won," called Jane, "there's the brush!"

"It's not fair," wailed Lupin. "I was busy."

They all gazed at one of the wire brushes, as it woggled about above a chimney pot.

"Now, when it goes, after a little wait, we'll go in, and he will have finished," Vanessa said.

But the brush didn't go. There it stayed, high above them, looking a little forlorn. In the end it even stopped moving.

"It isn't waving any more," said Lupin. And she waved at the brush, to encourage it.

"Perhaps he's forgotten it. Come along, no doubt he's finished. Follow me."

Vanessa led the way in at the back, and threw open the dining-room door.

There was nobody there.

"Strike me pink," said the parrot in muffled tones.

"Gone up to the parlour, no doubt," she said.

They trooped upstairs. In the parlour there were two brushes, but no sweep.

"Bless my soul," Vanessa said. "Perhaps he was a burglar in disguise."

"You could see the disguise," said Lupin.

"A cat burglar!" went on Vanessa.

"If he was a cat burglar," said Amanda, "why hasn't he taken the kitten?"

For the kitten sat on the hearth, looking at the empty grate.

"That's not what it means, you ignorant doll. It means a burglar who climbs all over the place, in at windows, and so on, like a cat."

"Vanessa, I wonder if he's climbed up the chimney," said Jane.

The kitten arched his back, stepped into the grate, and put his paw up to the hole.

"He's telling us," said Elizabeth.

Vanessa kneeled down.

"Sweep!" she called. "Where are you?"

"I'm stuck," answered a dismal and muffled voice.

"Did you hear? I notice he can speak when he's stuck. What are we to do? He's very thorough, he's climbed up and got stuck. He should have used a boy, like I said."

"Or the kitten."

"The kitten's done it before."

"Get the tongs and see if we can pull his feet," Elizabeth suggested.

They did this, Elizabeth lying in the grate and putting her arm up the chimney. She seized something with the tongs and pulled.

"Ow-w-w!" wailed the voice.

"Well, what *does* he want?" Vanessa snapped.

They pulled, and pulled, but no sweep appeared.

"My goodness, he *is* stuck," said Vanessa. "I suppose the paying-guest has not been pouring glue down the chimney?"

"I know," Amanda said, "I'll get on the roof by the fire-escape, and push the brush."

And she ran off to do so. Lupin ran to watch her. Not long after this there was another howl, more dismal than the first.

"We can't help it," Vanessa called. "We can't have you there forever, how are we to light any fires, unless we burn you," she finished, snorting.

Elizabeth got her head and shoulders into the grate. She could reach better this way. She stretched her arm up, and felt some feet. She grasped one, very hard. It was easier than the tongs. She pulled with all her might. There were groans and pants and grunts and muffled words.

The foot began to move.

"It's coming," she said.

Then there was a rustle and a sliding noise, Elizabeth ducked out, and two large fawn feet appeared. All the black robes had been left behind, and it was obvious who it was. Vanessa looked outraged.

"It's not the sweep at all, it's the monkey," laughed Jane.

"It serves you right," Vanessa said sternly. "I suppose you thought we'd been taken in."

"You was," the monkey said, dusting himself down, and collecting his brushes. He felt better now that he was out.

"You mean 'you *were*.' Really, the grammar of this animal!" Vanessa said.

"I don't mean that I were, I mean you was," said the monkey, grinning.

Vanessa stumped across the room, feeling muddled herself.

Amanda ran in laughing. "I thought it was the monkey, because he wasn't on the roof," she said.

"Six and sixpence each chimbley," the monkey announced, holding out his large hand. "Fifteen shillings the two," he added quickly.

The boldness of it!" said Vanessa. "And all

that disguise left in the chimney, blocking the flues—I never heard such nonsense, you shall not have a penny."

"I don't want a penny," he said. "I wants fifteen shillings."

Lupin went to the teapot where the rent was kept and gave him a cough drop.

"There you are, fifteen exactly," she said.

"And now be off!" said Vanessa. "And Lupin can make the tea, dear Mrs. Small. We all deserve it, but we can't possibly ask the sweep to tea," she whispered, "such ladies as we all are."

The monkey ran down the stairs, sucking his cough drop, and chuckling.

"We ought to have offered him a cup," said Jane.

"He can have it on the roof," Vanessa said, and closed her mouth with a snap.

VIII

EASTER EGGS

IT was Easter. Elizabeth had had chocolate eggs and marzipan eggs, hollow eggs and stuffed eggs, eggs with chocolates in them, and tiny, speckled birds' eggs, made of sugar, laid in a nest of moss with violets round it. And she had had new hair ribbons of pretty colours, and a fluffy yellow chicken. So she chose some of the

things for the dolls' house, and put them ready
in the garden.

As she walked up the path she saw the new
flowers she had got for the dolls: there were two
little rows of wooden flowers, painted prettily,
daffodils and hyacinths; and there was a clump
of primroses and a bundle of violets off somebody's old hats. She thought they looked very
nice.

The monkey peered at her from the roof.

"'The flowers that bloom in the spring tra-
la,'" he began to sing, in a very funny voice.
Elizabeth laughed: the monkey's voice was even
funnier than Vanessa's.

"I always meant to ask you," she said, "why
you fought those Zoo monkeys?"

The monkey looked shy.

"They said I was stuffed," he grumbled.

"Well, so you are, aren't you?"

"An' I said they was blockheads."

"Quite true, wooden. You're different makes.
But I can't see that's any reason for fighting,"
said Elizabeth, who had been brought up not to.

"So we comes to blows," he finished, "and I
won."

At this moment the dolls' house door opened
and the dolls streamed out.

"We saw you talking," cried Jane.

"We heard you coming," added Amanda.

"We guessed it was you," said Lupin.

"My dear landlady, we must show you the garden——" began Vanessa.

"A happy Easter!" said Elizabeth to them all. "It's Easter, you know!"

"Why, bless my soul, so it is!" said Vanessa. "Fancy my losing sight of that! I might have known, with all these delightful flowers coming out in the garden! That explains it!"

"They're lovely, Mrs. Small," Jane said, seizing her hand. "There's a whole row of daffodils——"

"And some hyacinths——" said Amanda.

"But they're not very high. I'm higher than they are," Lupin protested.

"Ridiculous doll, it's not that kind of high. And some primroses, Mrs. Small, rather large, more like ordinary roses, but never mind——"

"And we love the violets," Jane added, "they've grown in a bunch."

"Isn't that clever? But we shan't pick them. The strange thing is," Vanessa went on in her loud whisper, "these flowers are never in the same place two days running (not that days run, of course, so it's all nonsense) ."

Elizabeth realized that she had moved the

flowers about rather a lot, trying to find the best place.

"But we don't mind a bit, it makes a change and is most remarkable. We never know where they'll be next."

"And yet they don't seem to mind," said Jane, bending down to smell the violets which today were in the front.

"A lovely scent," she said.

"Let me," said Lupin.

"Dear Jane likes to imagine it, but I smelt nothing," whispered Vanessa.

"What does nothing smell like?" asked Lupin.

Vanessa looked puzzled and cross and changed the subject.

"Well now, if it's Easter, as Mrs. Small says, and she usually knows, there are all kinds of things as well as flowers. For instance, we ought to have had hot cross buns——"

"Why are they cross?" Lupin said.

"Perhaps you'd be cross if you were going to be eaten. But it's not that sort of cross at all— dear me, Mrs. Small, I can see I shall have to continue their education, or send them to Sunday School. And then," she went on quickly, "there's Easter bonnets and Easter cakes——"

"And Easter eggs," said Elizabeth.

"And Easter cards," said Jane.

"But what's the good if we haven't got any of them," said Lupin sadly.

"I've brought some," Elizabeth said, "and we can make the rest."

"Certainly. Make do and pretend," said Vanessa. "Now, who'll do what?"

"I know what I'll do," Jane said, running inside.

"And so do I," said Vanessa following her.

"And I'm going to hide some things in the house and garden," said Elizabeth, "for everybody to find."

Jacqueline said nothing, but slipped away upstairs.

"Now, you two——"

"I don't know what we've got to do," Lupin said.

"We'll hide things, too, like Mrs. Small!" said Amanda. "Come on, Lupin, I understand!"

Elizabeth was not sure that Amanda did understand, but at least the two youngest dolls seemed busy. She met them on the stairs and in the kitchen, and by the stable, as she scampered round hiding Easter eggs and ribbons. They giggled and hid things under their clothes.

Vanessa was in her bedroom.

"Oh, don't look, don't look, Mrs. Small!" she said.

"I'm not looking," said Elizabeth, but she could not help seeing the scrap-box.

"And don't you look either," she said as she hid an egg beneath Robin's pillow.

Vanessa bent her head quickly, but there was a smile on her face all the same.

Jane was in the parlour, at the table. She covered things with her arm as Elizabeth came in.

"All right, I'm not looking, Jane. What's the matter with the parrot?" Elizabeth asked. "He's standing in the corner of his cage with his back to me."

"I know, Mrs. Small, he's been like it for several days, we don't know what it is. Vanessa says he's broody," Jane whispered.

"Or moody," said Amanda, dancing in at this moment.

"Or greedy," added Lupin, "because he stands over his seed tray all the time."

"Or seedy," said Elizabeth without thinking. "That means ill," she added.

"I hope he's not ill," said Lupin. "Mrs. Small, can you make him better? He hasn't said anything for days and days." Lupin's eyes were round with anxiety.

"Usually he says things whenever we go in," added Amanda.

"We'll see what we can do after we've finished Easter," Elizabeth said. And she ran off to make a little nest by the skating-rink. She put sugar eggs inside it and sat the yellow chicken on top.

"Mrs. Small!" called Vanessa's voice from her bedroom window. Elizabeth stood up guiltily, and pushed the bulrushes back into place by the pond.

"Yes, Vanessa?"

"Is everyone ready?" demanded Vanessa.

"I am," said Jane, running out on to the back lawn. She looked pleased with herself.

"Ready for what?" said Amanda.

Vanessa thought for a moment. "Can you suggest what?" she said to Elizabeth. "What we're all ready for?"

"Ready, steady, go," remarked the monkey.

"But go where?" Amanda asked.

"I know, exactly," Elizabeth began. "We all hunt for the things I've hidden——"

"And I've hidden," Amanda said.

Lupin was not there.

"And when we've found everything, we all

have tea on the lawn, and the cake can have a new ribbon as it's Easter."

"Excellent," Vanessa said. And Amanda laughed, looking mischievous. "And everybody," Vanessa called, making her hands into a loud-speaker and shouting, "every doll is to wear a new Easter bonnet! No bonnet, no cake!"

Jane looked worried.

"I haven't got one."

"Nor have I," said Amanda.

"Nor me," said the monkey.

"You were not invited," Vanessa called to him. "You must all turn to and find one, that's all," she said crossly. "I intended to make bonnets for all but I have only had time to do mine, so there it is." And she drew her head in, slammed the window and disappeared.

"Ready, steady, go!" cried Elizabeth. "And bring whatever you find to the tea party."

All the dolls scampered about, looking for the Easter eggs and the ribbons which Elizabeth had hidden. The monkey swung down from the roof, wearing a turban (it was his spotted cravat), Vanessa hurried out, and over to the skating-rink, Amanda and Jane disappeared to the front, and Jacqueline sat on the lawn, eating a sugar egg, and wearing a lace mat, which went very well with her best lace dress.

Meanwhile Elizabeth laid the tea.

"Mrs. Small," shrieked Vanessa, "the kitten is worrying this sitting bird!"

For the black velvet kitten had discovered the chicken and was arching his back and looking at it.

"So's old red cheeks," reported the monkey, "she's stealing the turkey's eggs! And she's looking at her new hat in the skating-rink!"

"Turkey," Vanessa snorted, blushing, "it can't be a turkey, you have turkeys at Christmas, not Easter." And she tossed her head and put her hat straight, as if she wanted people to notice it.

"Tea's ready," said Elizabeth, "except that I can't find the teapot! Oh, and Vanessa, where's the cake?"

"In its usual place, no doubt," Vanessa said, heaping sugar eggs in a pile. "Come along," she sang.

At this moment Jane came round from the front.

"Splendid, dear Jane, if a little big, and I hope it won't kill them."

Elizabeth laughed. Jane was wearing the violets for her bonnet. She came forward, curtsied carefully, and stood an Easter card on the lawn by the food. It was a charming card. It had flowers drawn and painted all over it and inside it said: "A Happy Easter to us all." Jane had done it with her quill and the paints.

"Jane!" said Elizabeth. "How pretty!"

"So it is, so it is," Vanessa said. "I always said Jane was the cleverest, and I was right."

"And violets go very well with your dress," Elizabeth added. "Oh, look at Amanda!"

Amanda ran blindly round, holding her hat on with one hand and groping with the other. She had copied Jane, and was wearing the primroses. She was smothered.

"Not very fashionable," Vanessa sniffed, "and too old for you, Amanda."

"Yours is lovely," Jane said. "I seem to have seen it before."

Vanessa smiled and bowed. Elizabeth gazed at the bright green felt hat she wore. It was covered all over with little flowers and was a very curious shape.

"Or you can wear it this way," Vanessa said, proudly, turning it round. It looked like a bishop's hat.

"Vanessa!" screamed Elizabeth. "It's the tea-cosy!" It was really an egg-cosy which she had brought for the dolls' teapot.

"What if it is?" snapped Vanessa. "You've just said we've lost the teapot, so that doesn't need it——"

Amanda came out from under the primroses and said: "Ha, ha, he!"

"Where's the teapot, Amanda?" said Elizabeth.

"Lupin and me hid it."

"Then go at once and find it," Vanessa said.

"It's you that's got to find it. And the cake," Amanda explained.

"Ridiculous doll, you've got hold of the wrong end of the stick——"

"I haven't got hold of a stick at all," Amanda argued, "but if I had I know who I'd hit with it," she muttered.

"Anyway, there's plenty to eat without the cake," Vanessa said, taking no notice of this and pushing the tea-cosy further on. "And if we don't hurry the monkey and the paying-guest will have eaten it all. As it is they've been busy. What's this large brown egg, Mrs. Small?"

Elizabeth had put the chocolate cream egg in the middle, and was cutting it in slices.

"It's a pudding," said Jane.

"Whatever it is, it's delicious," Vanessa said, taking a large bite. "Come along at once, Lupin," she called, in a sticky voice, as the back door opened and Lupin ran out. "And where is your bonnet? We thought you had hidden yourself as well as the teapot."

"Vanessa, Mrs. Small, Jane, do come, it's so exciting, you can't think what I've been watching, what's happened, come quickly!"

They all rose up, holding on their hats, and ran into the house. Lupin led the way into the dining-room, and over to the gilt cage.

"The parrot!" she gasped. "The parrot's laid an egg."

In the corner of the cage lay a large white egg.

"Bless my soul!" Vanessa said.

"Isn't he clever?" said Lupin.

"Isn't she clever, you mean," Jane said.

"That proves he's a lady and not a man," screamed Amanda.

"*She's* a lady," Vanessa said. "Which is more than you are."

"Look, she's pleased!" said Jane.

The parrot side-stepped along her bar and winked.

"Bless my soul, bless my soul, strike me pink!" she said at last.

"That's the first time she's said anything for ages."

"No doubt this egg was on her mind. It's all this talk of Easter eggs has gone to her head. How very remarkable to be sure."

"Will it hatch?" Lupin asked with shining eyes. "Shall we have a baby parrot?"

"I very much hope not," Vanessa said. "One is quite enough, with all the words that monkey teaches it—her."

"Hoity-toity," remarked the parrot.

"Shall we put blankets over it, to keep it warm?"

"It ought to have a nest, you know," said Jane. "She had nothing to make a nest of, poor Polly."

"Hold the line, hold the line, hold the line," said the parrot.

"My word, she is talkative," said Vanessa, "it's a good thing she doesn't lay an egg every day, we shouldn't be able to hear ourselves think. Now, come along, and leave her in peace, she may want to hatch it, and anyway, all the Easter eggs will be gone if we leave the table too long."

This was very true: the monkey and Jacqueline had stayed behind, and the tea party looked a little bare. Lupin seized a piece of chocolate cream egg and started to chew.

"And I must go," Elizabeth said, "and I may not be able to come for quite a long time, be-cause——"

"And *we* may not be able to have you, dear Mrs. Small, because——" Vanessa answered.

"Because what?" Elizabeth said laughing.

Vanessa thought for a moment.

"Because of all these creatures," she explained. "The house and garden get fuller and fuller every minute. What with the monkey and Hugo his invisible friend, and Robin the baby, and the horses, and the kitten, and that yellow chicken, and what with the parrot having laid this egg, the place is becoming overcrowded."

"It's never too full for Mrs. Small," said Jane, holding her hand.

"No it isn't," said Amanda. "She brought us these lovely eggs."

"Good-bye!" they called as Elizabeth went. "We'll send a telegram if the egg hatches!"

"Good-bye!" said Elizabeth, waving.

And she left them all sitting on the lawn: Vanessa arranging her tea-cosy, Amanda and Lupin fighting over the last piece of egg, Jane trying to calm them, and Jacqueline smiling greedily to herself as she watched. The monkey had evidently gone back to the roof again to sleep things off, for he was nowhere to be seen.

THE END

The book you have read was first published in England. You may have noticed that the English spelling of some words is different from the American. The English, for example, spell color with a *u*—colour. The English meanings of words and phrases are sometimes different from ours as well. Below you will find the American meaning of some words and phrases in this book that may puzzle you.

GLOSSARY

Bath essence:	Bath salts
Bird-table:	A stand upon which food is placed for garden birds
Bodkin:	Dull needle with a large eye
Cotton:	Thread
Croquet hoop:	Wicket
Dumb show:	Pantomime
Knobbly:	Bumpy
Lorry:	Truck
Mouse-and-trap:	Mouse-and-buggy. A trap is a kind of cart.
Prick:	Shot or injection
Queuing up:	Lining up
Roundabout:	Merry-go-round

Screw packets:	Old-fashioned paper packages in which you put candy and twist the top
Skiffle group:	A group of young people who play popular music with unusual instruments
Smuts:	Floating specks of soot
Stone:	An English measure of weight, equalling 14 pounds
Sweep:	A man who cleans out chimneys
Treacle:	Molasses
Wooden brick:	Toy block

Other *FIVE DOLLS* books by Helen Clare

Published:

FIVE DOLLS IN A HOUSE
FIVE DOLLS AND THE MONKEY
FIVE DOLLS IN THE SNOW

Coming:

FIVE DOLLS AND THE DUKE

HELEN CLARE is the pen name of Pauline Clarke, the well-known English author. She has written many books for children under both names.

Her book *The Twelve and the Genii,* won the 1962 Carnegie Award in England. It is called *The Return of the Twelves* in its American edition.